Welcome to
The Giggle Club

The Giggle Club is a collection of picture books made to put a giggle into early reading. There are funny stories about a contrary mouse, a dancing fox, a turtle with a trumpet, a pig with a ball, a hungry monster, a laughing lobster, an elephant who sneezes away the jungle and lots more! Each of these characters is a member of **The Giggle Club**, but anyone can join: just pick up a **Giggle Club** book, read it and get giggling!

Turn to the checklist on the inside back cover and tick off the Giggle Club books you have read.

TEE HEE!

HA HA!

The Big Wide-Mouthed Frog

A Traditional Tale

illustrated by
ANA MARTÍN LARRAÑAGA

WALKER BOOKS
AND SUBSIDIARIES
LONDON • BOSTON • SYDNEY

Once there was a big wide-mouthed frog with the biggest, widest mouth you ever did see.

And one day that
big wide-mouthed frog
hopped off to see the world.

The first creature he met had
big thumping feet.

"Hey, you! Big Thumping Feet!
Who are you and what do you eat?"
shouted the wide-mouthed frog.
"I'm a kangaroo," said Kangaroo, "and I eat grass."
"Well, I'm a big wide-mouthed frog!"
shouted the wide-mouthed frog.
"And I eat flies!"

The second creature
he met had a big
black nose.

"Listen, Mister Big Nose!
Who are you and what do you eat?"
shouted the wide-mouthed frog.

"I'm a koala," said Koala,
"and I eat leaves."
"Well, I'm a big wide-mouthed frog!"
shouted the wide-mouthed frog.
"And I eat flies!"

The third
creature
he met
was
hanging
upside
down.

"Ho there,
Upside-down Creature!
Who are you and what do you eat?"
shouted the wide-mouthed frog.
"I'm a possum," said Possum, "and I eat blossom."
"Well, I'm a big wide-mouthed frog!"
shouted the wide-mouthed frog.
"And I eat flies!"

The fourth creature he met had
three long toes.
"Look here, Three Long Toes!
Who are you and what do you eat?"
shouted the wide-mouthed frog.

"I'm an emu," said Emu, "and I eat grasshoppers."
"Well, I'm a big wide-mouthed frog!"
shouted the wide-mouthed frog.
"And I eat flies!"

Then the wide-mouthed frog met
a creature stretched out on the riverbank
like a knobbly brown log.

"HEY, Knobbly Brown Log!
Who are you and what do you eat?"
shouted the wide-mouthed frog.

Knobbly Brown Log opened her mouth in a slow, wide, lazy smile.

"Good-day to you, too," she said.
"I'm a crocodile and I eat
big wide-mouthed frogs.
Who are you and what do you eat?"

"Me?" whispered the wide-mouthed frog, puckering his mouth into the smallest, narrowest mouth you ever did see.

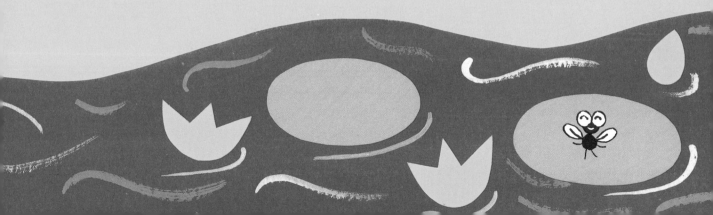

For Andrés

First published 1999 by Walker Books Ltd
87 Vauxhall Walk, London SE11 5HJ

10 9 8 7 6 5 4 3 2 1

Text © 1999 Walker Books Ltd
Illustrations © 1999 Ana Martín Larrañaga

This book has been typeset in ITC Highlander Book.
Printed in Hong Kong

British Library Cataloguing in Publication Data
A catalogue record for this book is available from the British Library.

ISBN 0-7445-6975-3

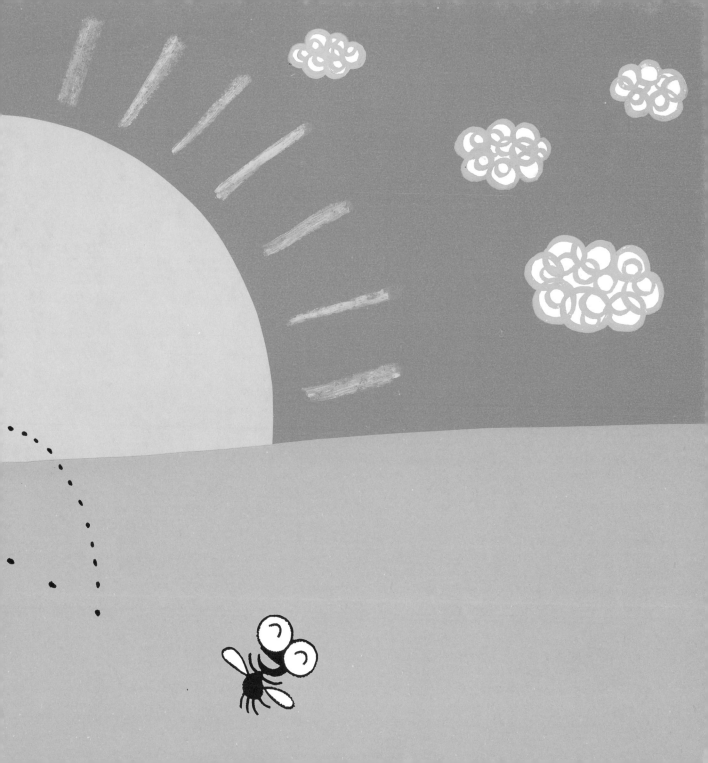